TWO is ENOUGH

TWO IS ENOUGH

by Janna Matthies

Illustrated by Tuesday Mourning

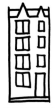

RP|KIDS

PHILADELPHIA • LONDON

ISBN 978-0-7624-5561-4
Library of Congress Control Number: 2014936260

9 8 7 6 5 4 3 2 1
Digit on the right indicates the number of this printing

Designed by Frances J. Soo Ping Chow
Edited by Lisa Cheng
Typography: Archer, Harman Deco, and Helvetica Neue

Published by Running Press Kids
An Imprint of Running Press Book Publishers
A Member of the Perseus Books Group
2300 Chestnut Street
Philadelphia, PA 19103–4371

Visit us on the web!
www.runningpress.com/rpkids

For Carter and his beautiful mom, Christine
On the night you were born, full of shimmer and swoon,
I knew you were mine, like the earth knows the moon.

—J.M.

To Ez and to Audrey,
whose joyful families inspire me

—T.M.

Two is enough
for a snowball fight,

For building a family,
frosty and white.

Two is enough
for an ice-skating show,

For towing toboggans,
for "ready-set-go"!

Two is enough
for unzipping suits,

For high-fiving mittens,
for tugging off boots.

Two is enough for a warm-you-up hug,
For toasting hot chocolate, mug against mug.

Two is enough
for scattering seeds,

For giving bouquets and
a necklace of weeds.

Two is enough
for refreshing the nest,

For a sweep and a shine
so it's looking its best.

Two is enough
for a rainy-day ride,

For singing duets with
our mouths open wide.

Two is enough for drying your tears,
For cuddling close till the storm disappears.

Two is enough
for a double-scoop treat,

For sand castle contests,
for splashing our feet.

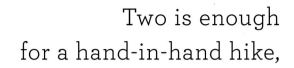
Two is enough
for a hand-in-hand hike,

For racing downhill
on a four-pedal bike.

Two is enough
for a thistledown wish,

For passing the ball
and playing Go Fish!

Two is enough for a cool *cha-cha-cha*,
For muffling your ears while we *oooh!* and we *aaah!*

Two is enough
for a back-to-school kiss,

For listening to stories
of moments we miss.

Two is enough
for crash-landing in leaves,

For carving a pumpkin,
for scare-crowing sleeves.

Two is enough
for a marshmallow roast,

For telling the knock-knocks
that tickle us most.

Two is enough, when the candles are blown,
For marking the doorframe to see how you've grown!

In winter and spring,
in summer and fall,

I love you! I love you!
I love you through all!

Sure as one plus one will always be two,
Two is enough when it's me plus you!